Time

Illustrated by Colin Twinn

The weather clock says

9 o'clock

Today is Susan's birthday. She has lots of presents to open.

The grandfather clock says

10 o'clock

The postman has arrived. Susan
hopes there will be some birthday
cards for her.

The kitchen clock says

11 o'clock

What a busy time in the kitchen!
Polly is helping Mother make a cake.

The kitchen clock
now says

12 o'clock

It's lunch time. Mother
has to finish
decorating the cake
before she is ready.

The church clock says

1 o'clock

'Look at the time,' says Father.
'We must hurry if we don't want
to be late.'

The station clock says

2 o'clock

The train's on time. Granny is here for Susan's party.

The living-room clock says

3 o'clock

Susan and her friends have 15 minutes to hunt the thimble. Father is timing them with his stop-watch.

The wrist-watch says

4 o'clock

Susan is given a watch of her own for her birthday. Now she can always tell what time it is.

The birthday cake clock says

5 o'clock

The children play blind-man's buff to the music of Father's violin. Mother brings in the cake for tea.

The grandfather clock says

6 o'clock

The party is over and it's time to say goodbye. Susan's friends have balloons to take home with them.

The alarm clock says

7 o'clock

It is getting late. Time for Tom and Harry to go to bed.

8 o'clock
Goodnight!